# The Tired Bumble Bee

## Written and Illustrated by

# Amal M. Nassir

Once, I found
A bumble bee
Who staggered and climbed
Onto my knee.

She looked so tired.

She looked so glum.

I let her climb

Onto my thumb.

I wondered why
She looked so tired.
I asked her why
And she replied,

"Ooh, I've been flying
From flower to flower
And sweet nectar
I did devour...

I collected pollen
For my hive.
I felt so free.
I felt alive!

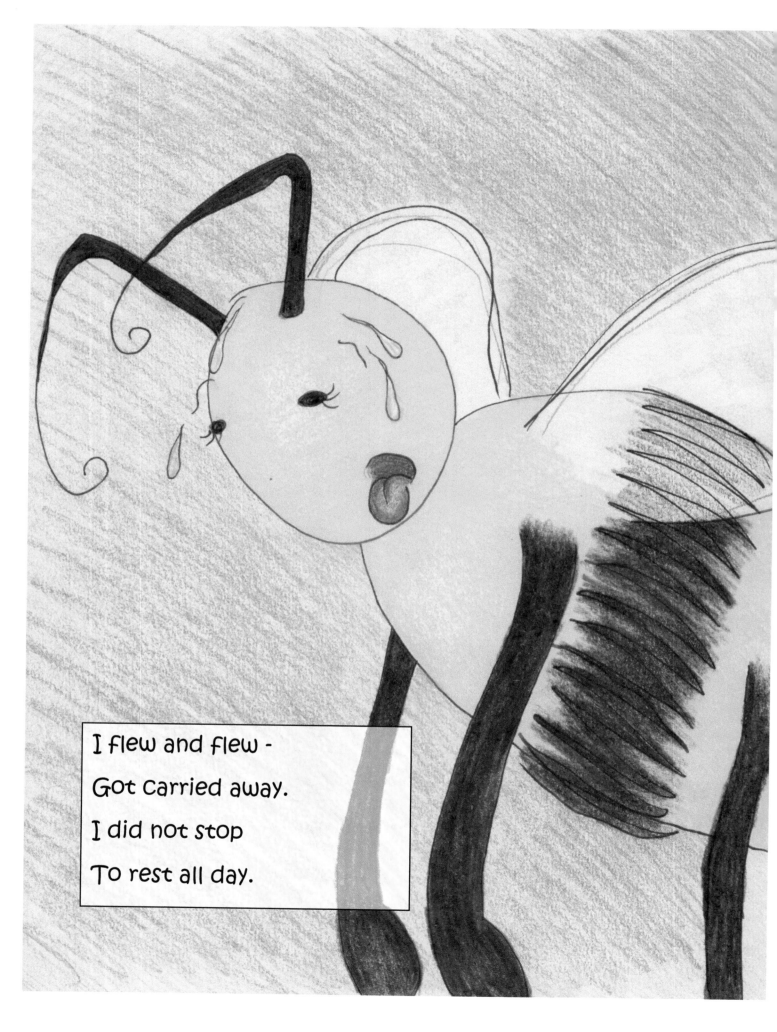

I flew and flew -
Got carried away.
I did not stop
To rest all day.

"Oh, tell me bee,
How can I help?"
She staggered, fell
And gave a yelp.

I gently placed her
On a rock,
And to my feet
I quickly got.

"Some Precious water,
I hear you say?"
Then, to the kitchen
I made my way.

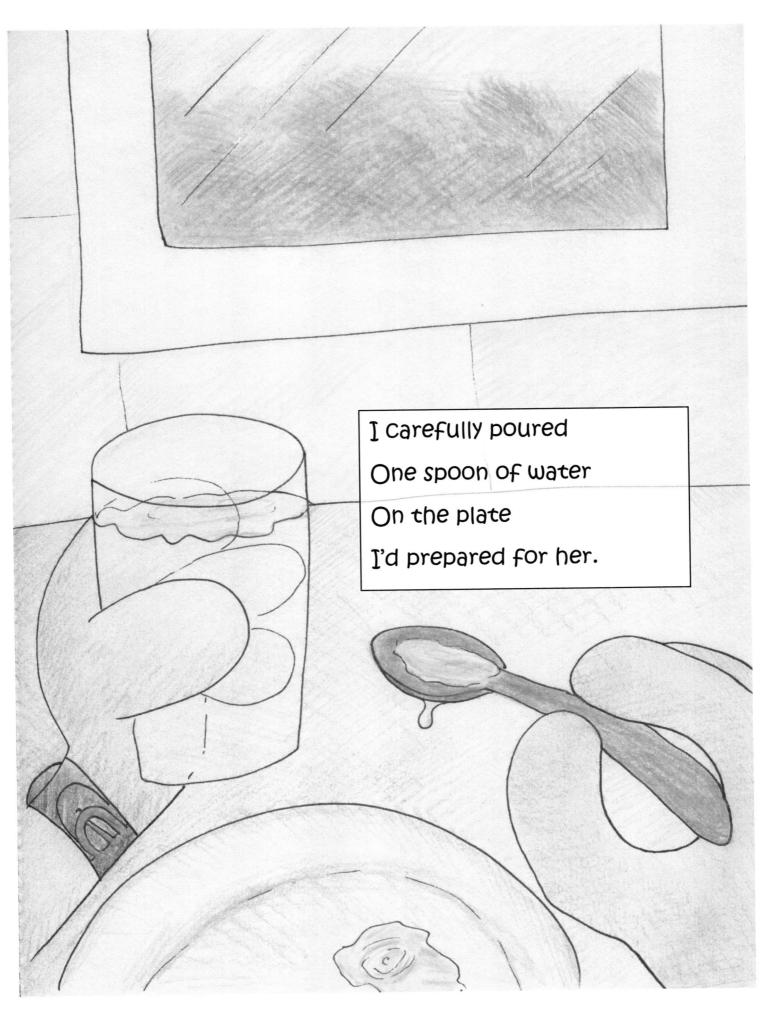

I carefully poured

One spoon of water

On the plate

I'd prepared for her.

She slowly climbed
Onto the plate
And then I watched her
Celebrate.

She drank and drank
And then she sighed,
"Oh, thank you so
For being kind.

Because of you,
I can, finally,
Go back and be
With my family."

She beat her wings
Then off she flew
And called out loud,
"I'll see you soon!"

I felt relieved

As I watched her fly

And fade away

Into the sky.

## Bees Are Friends

Did you know that bees are responsible for at least a third of the food that we eat?

Bees fly from flower to flower to collect nectar and pollen. Not only do they make some delicious, sweet honey which some animals rely on as food and medicine, they also help to pollinate the flowers.

By visiting many flowers, bees transfer pollen from one flower to the next. This helps the flowers to produce fruit, seeds and plants which other animals eat, disperse and rely on for shelter. Without them, our planet would be in danger – and us too!

Without bees, we would not have foods such as apples, oranges, strawberries, cucumbers, blueberries, cranberries, lemons and many, many more.

## "We need your help!"

Bees are in danger and they need your help!

People are destroying their habitat by building more and planting less.

Bees now have less food and are running out of safe places to build their hives.

Sometimes, people spray chemicals on plants which can kill bees.

## How can you help?

- Plant flowers that bees love, like rosemary and lavender.

- Watch out for the tired bees on the pavement (especially if it gets warmer).

- Build a mini-beast hotel for tired bees to rest safely.

- Help to spread the word to keep our bees safe and alive.

## About the Author

Amal M. Nassir is a mother and a primary school teacher with the passion for creativity and a need to make a positive difference to the children that she teaches.

Since a young age, she has expressed her imagination through her artwork and books. Amal enjoys oil painting, drawing and reading to her son, who (unsurprisingly) has also inherited her passion for books.

She hopes that her books will encourage positivity, kindness and compassion and has high hopes that the children of today will shape a kind, caring, compassionate and safe world tomorrow.

She is a firm believer that we all have the power to change the world, one kind act at a time. We just need to look for an opportunity.

# Other books by
# Amal M. Nassir

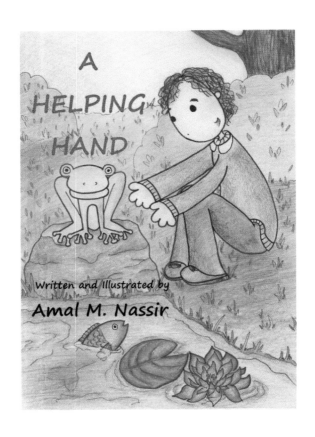

Available in paperback and as Kindle ebooks

Printed in Great Britain
by Amazon